The Poem of Ishmael

Christian Niemeyer

Copyright © 2021 Christian Niemeyer

214 Old Hickory Boulevard

Nashville, Tennessee 37221

All rights reserved

The images in this volume were obtained from the internet after a search for free photographs. Unfortunately, the results of the search were mixed. Included with pictures in the public domain were others restricted by ownership. When restriction was clear, payment to the owner was made. However, the provision of a few other pictures was not clear, and use was made with trepidation. No copyright infringement was intended. Most of the pictures picked for use in the story were altered in Photoshop to fit the narrative.

It is only with the heart that one can see rightly;
what is essential is invisible to the eye.

Antoine de Saint-Exupéry,
The Little Prince

Ishmael

The Poem of Ishmael

1.

Call me Ishmael. He was a fool in the waters. He floated on a coffin at the hands of the great white whale. That was Bohem, ruler of the oceans. You see, I am a penguin, an emperor penguin, mark that, floating on the ice in a cold tomb. I like the name Ishmael.

I have always been different. I wake up in the morn, the slant of light over the hills, sun piercing the cold, touching the earth. I swim in the sea, a smooth flight in green light. I feed on the delicacies of the water and bask on the rocks. I do what other penguins do. We live and die, but they, the others are content. They fix their coats, flip their arms, strut, and gaze. They chatter and fight, swim, migrate, mate, and die. They are absorbed in the endless sequence of the cold tomb. It is life to them, but I am different. I look at my feet and wonder why short and webbed. I look at my flippers and wonder why heavy and unfeathered. I look at my world and wonder why cold and repetitious.

I look at my world and wonder why.

The birds live in paradise. They are not fixed and limited to the earth. They fly and soar in the sun above the tomb. They are free, even the seagulls. I knew Jonathan, you know, but I did like him—too pretentious. The Albatross is my favorite. What grace in the air! What peace and beauty! Oh, what I could do, what I could be, if I were an Albatross. I look at my body, my feet and flippers, and sigh. I sigh often, for my fate pushes me in the chest and forces out the breath. One sighs to relieve the pressure.

The Albatross is my favorite.

2.

In the evening I sit on my favorite rock still warm from the afternoon heat and watch the setting sun. How beautiful the light stretching out across the land, resting on each stone, each blade of grass aglow, clear, every shape, golden. All becomes beautiful and clean in the sun, and the community of penguins rests comfortably. I love it when the world is lit, but the dark shadows creep up. The cold sets in the crevices, and the objects around me blur together, lost in the darkness.

As the last pale light disappears on the horizon over the empty sea, I fade too. I am nothing in the night of the cold tomb. I open my mouth to the air, pull up my flippers, stand erect, and scream, the only sound across the plain. It echoes through the hills and is lost on the sea. The others shift and rustle, small cackles in imitation. Eyes blink and dose back to rest. I am awake and alone.

One time I was swallowed by Bohem, several years back while we were feeding on a glorious patch of kelp deep beneath the cold surface of the sea. Out of the void Bohem charged, a huge dark form looming before us, his mouth gaping, a deep black cavern. He swallowed us all, all the helpless ones. One by one I watched them die around me, my friends, my noble penguins, and I cried, the only time I have ever cried, for the meaninglessness of it all. But the sickness of Bohem, it seems, caused him to belch me up, death parts and all, back to the world to see the land again.

Out of the void Bohem charged.

Alone at night, when the rest are comfortably sleeping, I do not cry, but I think of Bohem. I stare into the deep darkness of the West and feel I can be an interpreter.

3.

At noon when the breezes move across the land and the sun warms the back of the neck, I like to strut up the hill to my favorite spot on the mount, to look down on the community, the heads bobbing, chattering, hundreds upon hundreds caught up in the daily activities of living, movement everywhere in the peaceful stretches of the land. Out across the plain, the sea with waves and whitecaps stretches as far as the eye can see. There, on the horizon, where the birds fly far away, I gaze and ponder what it all means to come into this life by the sea. The birds and penguins, are they all accidents that live to die, superfluous seeds blown by winds across the rocks? Looking beyond the waves, past sight to the unknown, in the light afar, I search for the answer.

I am more than earth amd water.

But below, scattered about among the barren rocks are the bones, the white bones of penguins past. The bones bleached, and broken. I blink and raise my beak. I am an emperor penguin, an emperor. This life is not befitting, this endless struggle to live. I am not meant merely to survive. There must be more. I yearn for more. I am an emperor. I puff my chest, the white coat full, raise my flippers. Hear, O wind! Carry my sound to the sky. I am more than earth and water. I scream like the gulls, stamp my feet, and rock back and forth. To fly above the sea, to fly like the Albatross. To fly—

It is quiet in the afternoon. The wind slides down the hill, and I am fixed on rock. I look below and blink. The community is sleepy in the sun, and slowly I move off the mount, wending my way down to them.

4.

Morning feeding is a happy time, a refreshing swim in the ocean, curling in spirals under the sea, chasing, dodging, nudging friends in merry games, teasing the females who swim by with friendly eyes, resting in the waves as they swell and fall in gentle rocking. Full on kelp, I drift in idle daydreams under the blue sky, floating in the warmth of the sun.

I drift in idle daydreams.

Suddenly, the terrible cry of sea lions, the cry that chills the heart. In a mass we rush for the shore, our hearts pumping as we strain against the sea for our lives, shooting out of the water onto the rocks. I reach the ground and turn. It is terrible. Bodies on bodies, slipping, tripping, caught by the waves and tossed back like pebbles, caught in the undertow, crushed on the rocks. I stare in horror, frozen. And the sea lions wreaking havoc. Screams of penguins bit and slaughtered, blood in the sea, bodies no more, no more. One huge sea lion is out of the water, the massive body coming after me.

One huge sea lion is out of the water, the massive body coming after me.

I am more than earth and sea, I cry, more than earth and sea. I am an emperor. I grab a sharp shell in beak and face the loathsome lion, the stench unbearable. I strike his face with my flippers. Mouth open, he lunges. The shell! I thrust it forward as he snaps. It sticks in his mouth, cuts deeply, and blood pours forth, but not without cost. He has caught my flipper, a sharp pain travels down my back. My arm goes limp, and I fall into the sea. I feel dizzy. The waves carry me to the rocks, lifting me up above the jagged points, pulling me back just before I land on them. The sound is deafening, water crashing on the shore, and then the final thrust of sea and down on the rocks I come, my head striking hard, a dull pain. All goes black, like the deep darkness of the West.

5.

At midnight I wake. Slowly, I open my eyes to the night, a clear night with a bright white-yellow moon. I am lying on the pebbles behind the rocks, and I cannot move. I am stiff. The damaged flipper is numb, and my head aches. I see the bones among the rocks and shudder. Is this all? Is this all it comes to? Across the plain the community of penguins are at peace. I can hear their slumbering noises, for the day's events are past to them. It is time to live. They have forgotten me already in their comfortable sleep. I am no more in the land of the cold tomb. The emperor is gone. I open my beak to scream, but no sound comes forth. I feel cold. My eyes water. There must be more than this. There must. I call for more. Oh wind of sky, tell me of more than earth and sea. Oh bright moon, tell me before I die.

Oh bright moon, tell me before I die.

But the sky is no longer clear. A fog has moved in off the sea, and the moon casts an eerie light through the swirling air. It is quiet, so quiet even the waves seem still. Suddenly, a strange sound comes through the fog, a rushing wind, unlike wind, but rushing, rushing. My eyes grow large, for there above a shadow, a sweep, in the light through the fog, of, I think, of the Albatross, what majesty and grace! And it seems, though I am still in a daze, perhaps dreaming, it seems I hear a sweet voice in light music tell me, "Ishmael, Ishmael, fulfill thy nature and live." The sound fills me with joy, flooding me with warmth, and I sleep, dreaming peacefully of my mother when I was a child.

For there above a shadow, a sweep in the light through the fog, I think, of the Albatross, what majesty and grace!

END OF THE FIRST PART

6.

What tricks our minds can play. It is the middle of the day, and for some precious moments I feel my mother by my side, bending over as she straightens my coat, removes the sticks and sand. It is not my mother, but a young female, bending over quietly to care for me. Her touch is healing, and the gift is a wonder to me. Out of nothing, a presence to fill the heart, my heart. What an exciting mystery. How can it be, this fullness for me, in the empty world? The sun behind her casts a white light around her head, and she stands close, keeping me warm with her fur. As she looks up to gaze afar, erect, her white coat puffed, she looks a queen, a queen.

A young female, bending over quietly to care for me.

In the evening she moves away, her body heat gone, and the coldness I feel is worse. The stones are all I see in the cold tomb, and my wounds ache. I am too weak to move. I wonder whether I will ever see the morn again. I think of her touch, her dignity, and lo, she is there again. My heart beats faster. I move a flipper. She has brought me a fish to share, and I eat. It is good. It is good.

Later at night in the soft light of the moon, while all sleep quietly, I slowly follow Asenath to a quiet place near the rocks and there fall into a deep rest.

7.

Alive! The morning sun, fresh and white, heats the stones in the nest, and I rise to contemplate the light in the world of stone, earth, and sea. In spite of the cold, it is warm and bright. I rise, stretch my head and puff my chest to receive the sun. I feel its glory in my heart and fill with joy.

A head peeps over the rocks, two smart eyes twinkle and blink. Asenath is looking for mischief. She struts up to me, clamps my beak between her flippers, and playfully shakes my head. Then she spins around onto her belly and slides down the hill on the snow, scooting in and out of the rocks towards the sea. I give chase, chattering in the throat. At the bottom of the hill, Asenath shoots out over

I gave chase, chattering in the throat.

the rocks into the sea and disappears beneath the waves. Following, I soon find her near the bottom of the bay, spinning over and under the plants. I nip at her feet and brush the ocean floor. What dizzy clouds of ocean dust, twirling, swirling, we lose ourselves in, the heart beating faster and faster, ready to burst like light. We are close, and the sea is soft and green forever.

Later in the day, under the deep blue sky, I take Asenath to my place on the mount. We slowly move up to the high rocks and stand there quietly, looking out over the ocean, the breezes blowing softly to ruffle our coats. Water everywhere, blue water with white caps stretching to the horizon, teaching one of the immensity of the world of earth and sea. Alone on the mount, we face the future of life, on the gray rocks. As the sun sinks red into the cold sea, the dark shadows stretching

Alone on the mount, we face the future of life.

across the nests below, Asenath moves her feet and blinks. I too feel a tightness in the chest. The night comes, cold radiating up from the ice, and I touch her flipper, warm. There will be a sunrise in the morn.

8.

Life changes all around, but to find ourselves in the change is new, exciting. Anxiously we make the preparations, feeding in earnest now, for there is no time to play. We often puff our chests and scream to the world to warn the careless and the dangerous to stay away. We are serious, our foreheads furrowed for the time.

And in the night after the world has withdrawn in stillness, leaving us to huddle under the stars, Asenath gathers courage to give birth, a new life hidden in the egg, from nowhere a new presence, whole, round, beautiful. Asenath stands and

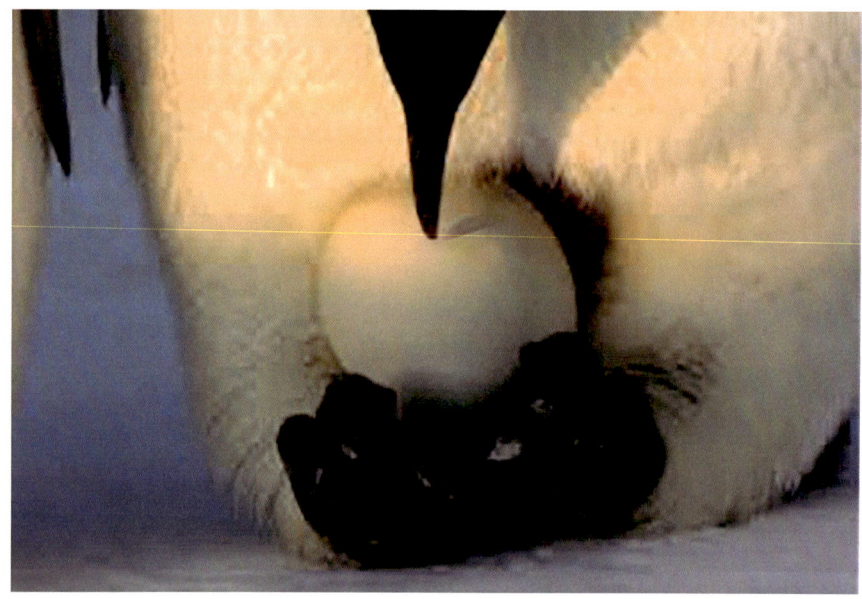

A new life hidden in the egg, from nowhere a new presence, whole, round, beautiful.

shakes her coat. She is proud and her eyes glow. She says nothing but quietly communes with what she has accomplished. I feel full, loving the place I am in. It confuses me to think perhaps the rocks and hills and sea are more to me than a place of weary struggle and defeat. How is it possible, this life within the tomb?

In the days of activity, we work to preserve the new one in the nest. I feed two weeks in the sea while Asenath sits, keeping the egg warm alive. Then trading places, she quietly disappears over the ice into the water, and I watch, sitting day and night, worried whether she will return but confident in my heart of the ache we have to keep our chick alive. It binds us together mysteriously, one life given to growing. She will return. Sitting there, looking over the busy community of penguins among the rocks, all sitting on eggs, I think I understand their contentment. There is something to the endless sequence of the tomb.

9.

What has changed? What is different? I still see earth and water, sea lions, and Bohem, still the bones among the rocks. The bones. They make sitting and feeding seem all for naught. Ishmael's coffin! Looking at the bones, I feel foolish to be content with the round egg, and I become lonely. I search the clouds. To see the limits of the earth and understand! If I could fly above, above with the birds, I would be free of the mysteries and the burdens, free in flight to see, to see! Up! I yearn, rocking back and forth, cackling impatiently, lifting my flippers as if to fly. Oh, I can feel it, up, up, high, free.

Yet there is nothing for a penguin but stones and bones. My heart slows, still, and I sigh and blink. Perhaps there is nothing more than the burden.

At night the winds blow the chilling mist and sitting is hard. I think of the warm sea and the abundant kelp fields at the bottom, swimming for food, floating in pleasure. But the round egg holds me. Somewhere in the heart, I do not understand. It is warm though I am cold, and its presence is life in the tomb. For the little one I will stay quiet within the dark.

A noise! The moon shines through the fog, beams of light in the swirling of the mist. A noise, that strange noise, rushing, rushing. My eyes widen, my beak opens. I remember! With my heart I call to the bird, the mighty bird. A shadow passes over, there again, in light and mist the sweep of grace. I am not dreaming, no. It flies high toward the mount. It moves in majesty, and through the endless white of fog I hear the enchanting summons, "Ishmael, Ishmael." Awake, I hear.

Strong night winds begin to howl, and I leave the egg to follow the bird up the narrow path, my coat blown out of place, my eyes squinting, blurred by tears. To the mount I struggle, flippers for balance, webbed feet over stone, but the vision of the bird is in front of me. Up, up, in the face of the storm sweeping in from the sea with huge thunderheads over the water, white foam in violence, and swirling clouds with cold black mist rolling over the earth, hiding the moon. Afraid, I keep on, to know the Albatross is all to me, though sleet pelts my coat, stings my face. Blinking through the dark, I come to the top, and there amidst flashes of lightning, the majestic Albatross stands, tall, wings outstretched, a form without a face.

"Oh Albatross, graceful Albatross," I breathe, and strange it all changes. A clap of thunder, lightning flash right on the mount, and the Albatross glows, a light all around like St. Elmo's fire. My eyes open wide. The face lights up, not like a

A clap of thunder, lightning flash right on the mount, and the Albatross glows.

bird, but sweet, beautiful, and I see into another world at peace. In the harmony of many voices, a full range of light cords and tender music, I feel, not hear, the bird speak.

"Ishmael, Ishmael, we have heard you. What is your cry?"

My throat is dry, but I can answer.

"To know, oh beautiful bird, to know what there is above earth and sea, to make sense out of this tomb so that I may be free from the endless cycle, the repetition that frightens me."

The face in sweetness floats, showering a light I do not see but feel in the heart, and rainbows cascade through and through, gold sparkles shimmering to my soul. "Know only this, oh bird of earth, that to seek the pure ideas of the air, to possess such freedom should not be your goal. The mind's possessions contain all the illusions of the earth. Alone they are empty, like the barren bones among the rocks."

I feel a pain inside, a tearing of the heart, ripped apart.

"Almighty Albatross, what does this mean? Is it true? What is left but earth and water. Is there nothing more?"

"Be wise, fleeting one. It is not what you know of the air but what you do with the life of earth that makes sense out of the tomb. The mind takes but the heart gives. A magnificent bird lives in the sunny South, the Pelican bird. Seeing starvation, it pierces its breast and gives its blood to the children for life."

"The Pelican bird pierces its breast and gives blood to the children for life."

"Pierces its breast to give blood?" I shudder at the thought and a fear possesses me. "The loss of life, oh Albatross. Our health, our wholeness, our gain given over, lost, without a battle. Such is death in the tomb. My death!"

The sweet face fills with light, overwhelms me, and tongues of flames burst out, flooding my heart. "I must leave you now, foolish one, for your own good in the sequence of things. Patience, be patient in the tomb, for a higher wisdom unfolds not in the musings of the mind but in the timely actions of the heart. Patience."

I am frantic. "Please, all seeing Albatross, please do not leave me. Explain the power of the sunny bird."

A silence follows, but the face remains, though with a more distant voice. "His power is great, to bring you to another, the greatest of all beyond the tomb, the Phoenix bird, who rises from the ashes of death with a new life ever and ever. Not ideas, little one, but the power of persons to give life forever."

"The Phoenix Bird rises from the ashes of death with a new life ever and ever.

For a brief moment I see all, harmony through and through, but the light dims, the glow disappears. Before me is a dark form, the tall bird reaching high with wings outstretched, and for a minute the moon appears through the clouds, casting the mighty bird's shadow across me. I hear the voice now from afar. "Live in this shadow, Ishmael, and find what you seek. Live in this shadow." Then it is gone.

"Live in this shadow, Ishmael, and find what you seek. Live in this shadow."

The night wind blows rain in sheets against my face, cold rain. I descend slowly, lost in the memory of the heart, not knowing what I have lived. Instinctively, as one blind, I make my way to the round egg, the place of life.

END OF THE SECOND PART

Oh relief! At our place I find Asenath there, protecting our precious egg. She stares at me, puzzled by my distant manner, and I walk up to her, close, and place my head against the side of hers, for a moment. It is quiet. I can hear our breathing. Asenath blinks and closes her eyes to sleep.

Later, in the silence of the night, under the moon clear and bright, with smells so fresh after the storm, huddling together, we witness our young one's birth to the world, a little male chick of fluffy down we named Ephraim. Soon after, the

We witness our young one's birth to the world, a little male chick of fluffy down we named Ephraim.

morning sun breaks ever over the horizon, red, pink light, then golden on the clouds and land, to warm the earth. I stand on the hill, puffed chest, raised flippers, and look across the wakening community of my friends, their life all around. Tears come to my eyes. It is a beautiful day.

With what care we now work to feed, to clean, to teach Ephraim how to live in the world of sea and land. He rises to our call, depends on our strength. Imitating us he learns to walk, following us for life, and we carry the awful responsibility of his future, for it is our instinct to do what is right to preserve his life.

We carry the awful responsibility of his future.

But always at the back of my mind is the dream-like memory of the magnificent Albatross who revealed a distant world far from me, removed from sea and land, in the air, it must be. And I envy that place and wonder about the earthly fate of the penguins, the birds who cannot fly and who can never meet the unbelievable Phoenix bird that lives again after the ashes. The Phoenix, what miracle of fire it has in contrast to our limited lives in the cold tomb. It thrills me to think of such a bird, but I feel a pang of sadness, deep, deep, to think it is not for me who has no wings.

12.

In the late afternoon when the sun's last heat makes the world lazy, still some hours before the evening breezes and the night winds, in the warmth we rest by the nest, the three of us, full on food, primmed and cleaned, comfortable in the hollows between the stones. And I think of the shape of Bohem, how odd, with a gangly tail, a tail with split fins, underdeveloped feet I guess, still a baby, and no beak, no beak, I chuckle. Mr. Bohem, the no-beak. Fellows, I give you Mr. No-beak. I start rocking in my hollow. Mr. No...

Suddenly terror, awake, screams of sea lions, and instant memories of helpless bodies, slaughter, blood, and bones among the rocks, the land of the tomb. I jump, all jump, everyone for himself, all is lost, given up, scrambling, running, slipping, falling, for the sea, away from the jaws of death, the monsters of doom.

I reach the rocks above the sea, mount to jump, flippers out, but I stop, stunned. On the rocks I see stretching out in front of me my shadow, the same shape, the same shape as the Albatross' shadow: "Live in my shadow, Ishmael, and find what you ask." A pang goes through my heart and instantly my mind's eye sees the strange bird of the sunny South that sacrifices its blood to save the children. Ephraim! My throat chokes. I cannot breathe. I turn and run toward Asenath, against the flow of penguins. I rush toward the sea lions. There I can see activity, Asenath against two, pushing Ephraim back behind her, back against the rocks.

Hurry Hurry! I am not fast enough. One lion grabs Asenath by the neck and shakes.

I can see the blood as she is hurled against the rocks, left there, fallen, lifeless. The other seizes Ephraim and heads for the sea. My stomach twists in pain. Asenath! Ephraim! Oh, Ephraim shrieking. My heart burns. Preserve the little life, the innocent one. My chest swells and head up, I scream to the sea lion. He turns on me, those cold eyes of death. I rush upon him, frantic, my beak ready, and stab deep into his neck, aware even then of the futility of it all, his huge body dominating the land.

But the unexpected happens. With a roar, a horrible noise that goes all through me, he drops Ephraim at the water's edge and strikes, catches me in the chest, leaving a gash on the right. I twist, push Ephraim into the sea, and dive into the wave.

Alone beneath the surface, alone! We have escaped in the cool green waters, a miracle, what miracle! In the endless quiet of the depths is gone, far away, the sea lion's harm.

13.

As I adjust to the dim light, my heartbeat slowing, a new fear hits me. Ephraim cannot swim. He is dropping down, down into the dark, the bottomless dark, it seems. There, over there. Sinking, his fluffy down floating around him. I

He is dropping down, down into the dark, the bottomless dark, it seems.

try to get under to push, to teach him the movements, but he only looks at me, helpless. Nothing works. I swim with him, tears in my eyes, pleading to the bird of rainbows, pleading for life.

Silence all around us as we enter the deep of the sea, calm, quiet, empty. I cannot see far in the murky water, I feel lost, but there, off in the distance it seems, a dark object moves, coming, coming toward us. Vague at first but then a large shape, larger, a huge wall moves. I see the massive form of Bohem, with mouth open, rushing upon us! We have no chance, no chance, we are swallowed whole together into the darkness, the darkness of our tomb.

Deep in the abyss the water recedes. Ephraim is unharmed, alive, in my arms. He snuggles for warmth and even there, in the guts of the leviathan, looking

Ephraim is unharmed, alive, in my arms. He snuggles for warmth in the guts of the leviathan.

into the sweet eyes of the young one, so trusting of his father, I feel an inner joy and peace, like the light of the Albatross, gold sparkles shimmering to my soul, and I ache to preserve the life of the little one, so fresh and innocent to the world. I touch his face softly with my flipper.

Hot tears well up, tears of shame for my fear, my wretched flight, my wretched flight to protect myself. I abandoned Ephraim and Asenath. Good Asenath lost. Her blood on my head. Heavy, so heavy the truth is to hold inside, to forsake her in fear of my life. Yes, it is just, this fate in the belly of the sea-monster. It is right, this darkness and this end for such an act, her faith, my betrayal. How bitter, that to save myself I sacrificed her life, our life, life itself. Ah, Albatross, how it hurts to see, the Pelican bird must be right. There is no other way.

Thinking of the sunny bird of the South, I gaze at my Ephraim, wishing he could have more than what I gave, more than what I gave. With my flipper around

Thinking of the sunny bird of the South, I gaze at my Ephraim, wishing he could have more than what I gave.

him, we drop off to sleep, I remembering the rainbows and sounds of light cords and tender music that seem now forever lost.

14.

The fear of death is nothing to the pain of loss, I think, holding Ephraim within the body of the leviathan. The preciousness of life, the beauty of living sits mysteriously in my heart, and Asenath gone, my fault even, crushes the heart, emptying the universe. But here still is Ephraim, his life won, by losing myself, like dying to save. Oh Albatross! The magic of the Pelican bird. How wonderful, to die for life, here this innocence still breathing, still living in the heart. Such joy! Your words are a breath of fresh wind. Like sailing through the air, I wonder about the Phoenix bird who rises from ashes to live again.

A rumbling shakes me out of thought, shakes me to the roots. I freeze. The end is here. The end, I fear, but I know now something better than earth and sea, something that transforms our life in the tomb. The end means less to me than—. Suddenly a wall of sea comes crashing down, tons of salt water to bury us. I hold Ephraim as we are pushed down, back to the end of the tunnel. It narrows, and we become wedged, stuck. I wiggle, flap, peck, fight hard. To save Ephraim, oh Albatross, to save Ephraim. All at once it is still, eerie, like the eye of a hurricane. We wait for eternity, wait. Then vibrations start, far away it seems, building, coming close, violent upheavals, wrenching and twisting in fury. In a horrible spasm we find ourselves thrust forward, dizzy, in blinding speed through the darkness, water and all. Losing track, I cannot see, it hurts, losing, losing, all goes dark.

15.

After the storm, the air is sweet. So it is as I wake, on a snowy plain by the sea, warmed by the sun and pleased by soft breezes. Around me are the friends and families I know so well. Oh joy of life, after winter spring! I am living, breathing, moving. Alive, alive! I stand on my feet, thrust my beak to the sky and flap, crying to earth and sea. We will live.

Alive, Alive! I stand on my feet, thrust my beak to the sky and flap, crying to earth and sea.

But I am alone. Ephraim. Ephraim! The silence holds nothing. Ephraim! I think of his young heart, innocent eyes, trusting, as he looked to me, and I think...of the white bones on the beach. My head hurts. I search the plain, the rocks by the sea, the hills above. Nothing. A tightening in my chest chokes my very life. He looked to me, he looked to me, and I could not help. Helpless, helpless. The evening comes, and the night mists swirl over the land. I cannot see. I cannot search. Pain in my forehead, my beak aches. "Oh Albatross, in your shadow I came to this point. Let not all be lost. Majestic bird, grant one more change in the land of earth and sea." My words mingle with the whirl of the wind, and all of a sudden my body gives out. I feel sleepy. I see a cave in the rocks and inside lie down to dream, to dream.

I am in mud, my feet fixed in the earth, and just there, from me, Ephraim is slipping away, looking to me with open eyes in fear, slipping, falling into a black void, more distant, far away, and my heart wrenches in unbelievable pain. My soul pleads, hurts, and then I am rising, tumbling, floating, in light. I discover a different place with bright faces around, looking at me, warm. A happiness fills my heart, for before me all white, completely white, is Asenath, her face, radiant, her eyes clear and shining with love so that I feel alive. Asenath, I call, but a new light floods me, brighter, brighter, not to the eye but to the heart so that I fall down in awe for what radiates through me, and in the midst of all a joy, a joy, for there I find the Albatross, my beloved Albatross, who cared for me in the land of earth and sea. He bends over me to raise me gently and then leads me into a pleasant room, a large chamber that fills me with peace so that I know I belong there and nowhere else, so full I feel, more than comfort, full. On a throne of stars sits a magnificent bird, red and gold. Yes, I know it is the Phoenix bird, so lofty my feet feel weak, and I ache for his approval. Next to the Phoenix is another, pure in white, with fresh blood on his chest that glows a beautiful red. The Pelican bird! I watch the Albatross speak to the Pelican, and I can feel lights like gold and white and silver and red flow through the room, weaving in beautiful circles and patterns. The Pelican turns to the Phoenix and seems to be pleading, peacefully. At the same time new intense red rays flow into the room, and we all feel earnestness, a sense of purpose, a new seriousness of the heart, deep, strong like a rock. Then all grows still, the lights almost pass away. Suddenly whiteness bursts from the Phoenix, pure whiteness strikes us as he stands and stretches his wings. I can feel a sound of power I cannot explain. The Albatross turns to me and for a moment I can see Asenath, smiling. In a second all vanishes.

The Albatross turns to me, and for a moment I can see Asenath, smiling.

I awake with a start. It is quiet, in the middle of the night, but my heart bursts, for there by my flipper, in the safety of the cave, breathing comfortably, stands my Ephraim!

For there by my flipper, in the safety of the cave, breathing comfortably, stands my Ephraim!

END OF THE THIRD PART

16.

The goodness of finding Ephraim I cannot describe. Reunited, we saunter back to our home on the rocks, returning to the familiar sequence of the tomb. But the world is not the same. A fire, a glorious fire burns in my heart for the power beyond the tomb, the sweetness of the sunny bird, changing, changing, giving newness to the old, warmth to the cold, life to the tomb. I feel tall, an emperor, in love with the special sequence that has brought me into the world, changed, changing with the sunny bird of life.

The seagulls, oh winged birds, how you are lost, separated from the sequence. Seeking your own heights, finding pleasures in flight, you know nothing of earth and sea, nothing of the monstrous sea lions, nothing of the heartaches, nothing of the white whale, until it is too late. Dear seagulls, you will never call on the Albatross, never call. Removed from the power beyond the tomb, you are so alone, and unchanging, unchanging. I shudder at the thought of that darkness, the void I once was. Oh, never to feel the rainbows in the soul. My seagulls, poor seagulls, so unfortunate to be born without webbed feet and unfeathered flippers. Descend, descend from the sky and learn to walk the earth.

Of course, here the rocks bruise the heels. We buried Asenath by our home, the place we once shared for birth. Her courage and dignity haunt me, and there is an emptiness in my heart without her, a pang every time I remember. And not long after, my beloved Ephraim left the nest for his life in the world, swimming off with

My beloved Ephraim left the nest for his life in the world.

other young to feed in warm seas. I felt then so alone, and yet in my heart was fixed the knowledge, the experience, that the power above the tomb will not be put out. Yes, there is more than the earth and sea, and no pain in the tomb can be greater than what is more, and will be, in the great change.

At night when the cold sets in the crevices, the many objects around me blur together, lost in the darkness, when the last pale light disappears on the horizon over the empty sea, I snuggle warm against the rocks of our place and drift off to sleep, dreaming peacefully of Asenath white in radiance, Ephraim, and the three in the rainbow. But somewhere in the night, across the sleeping community, I hear a scream, a sad cry that echoes though the hills. I open my eyes and sit for a while.

But somewhere in the night, I hear a scream, a sad cry that echoes through the hills.

Then slowly I rise, the winter wind cold on my stomach, and stiffly I make my way over the rocks to the young penguin standing erect with flippers stretched out under the bright moon. A fire burns in my heart.

CPSIA information can be obtained
at www.ICGtesting.com
Printed in the USA
LVRC100026190122
708888LV00012B/539